The Horse and the Colt

and other horse stories

Compiled by Vic Parker

Miles
Kelly

First published in 2014 by Miles Kelly Publishing Ltd
Harding's Barn, Bardfield End Green, Thaxted, Essex, CM6 3PX, UK

Copyright © Miles Kelly Publishing Ltd 2014

This edition printed 2016

4 6 8 10 9 7 5

Publishing Director Belinda Gallagher
Creative Director Jo Cowan
Editorial Director Rosie Neave
Senior Editor Claire Philip
Designer Rob Hale
Production Elizabeth Collins, Caroline Kelly
Reprographics Stephan Davis, Jennifer Cozens, Thom Allaway
Assets Lorraine King

ISBN 978-1-78209-453-1

Printed in China

British Library Cataloguing-in-Publication Data
A catalogue record for this book is available from the British Library

ACKNOWLEDGEMENTS
The publishers would like to thank the following artists who have contributed to this book:

Advocate Art: Simon Mendez (Cover)
The Bright Agency: Kirsteen Harris-Jones (inc. borders)
Frank Endersby (main illustrations)

Made with paper from a sustainable forest

www.mileskelly.net

Contents

The Horse and the Colt

By Jean Pierre Claris de Florian

*Fables are short stories that illustrate a life lesson or moral,
and they often feature animal characters. This horse fable comes
from a collection written by a Frenchman in 1792.*

THERE WAS ONCE a horse who didn't
know what it was like to be owned by
humans because he had always lived in the
wild. He lived with his son in a pretty
meadow, where the streams, the flowers

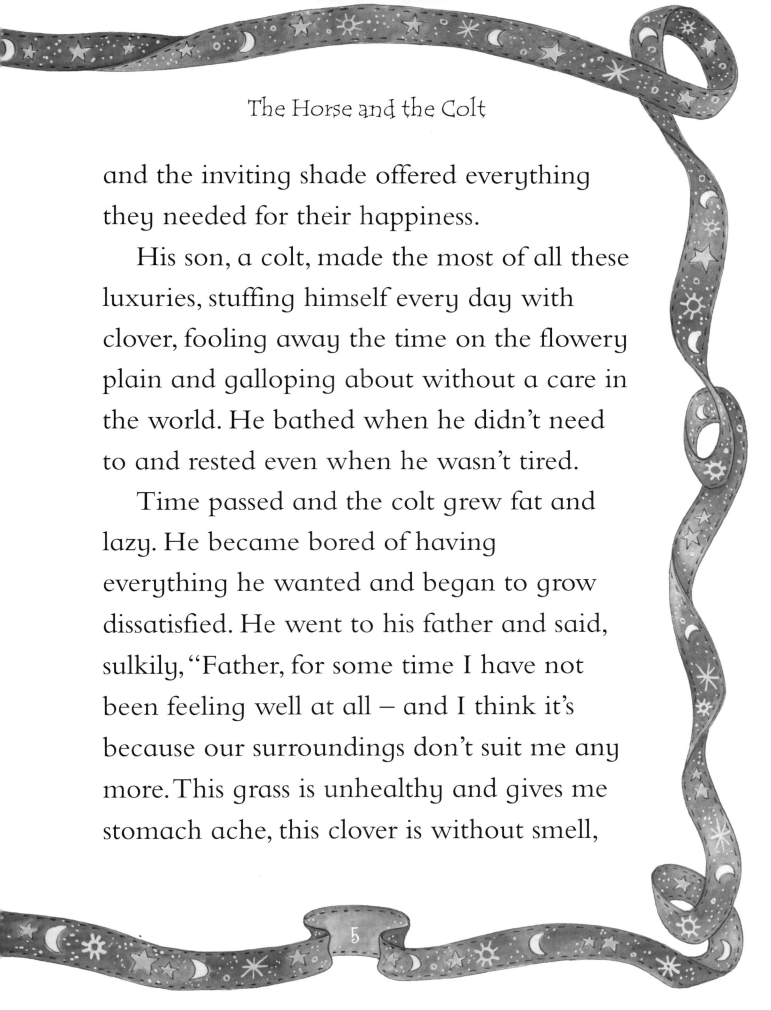

and the inviting shade offered everything they needed for their happiness.

His son, a colt, made the most of all these luxuries, stuffing himself every day with clover, fooling away the time on the flowery plain and galloping about without a care in the world. He bathed when he didn't need to and rested even when he wasn't tired.

Time passed and the colt grew fat and lazy. He became bored of having everything he wanted and began to grow dissatisfied. He went to his father and said, sulkily, "Father, for some time I have not been feeling well at all – and I think it's because our surroundings don't suit me any more. This grass is unhealthy and gives me stomach ache, this clover is without smell, this water is muddy, even the air we breathe here gives me a bad chest. In fact, I really think that unless we go elsewhere, I might get so ill that I may actually die."

The horse, his father, listened carefully and replied, "My dear son, that does sound truly dreadful. We must leave at once."

And as soon as he finished speaking he immediately led the colt off in search of a new home.

The young traveller neighed for joy, but the old one was less merry. He made his child clamber up a steep, dry mountain where there was no grass to eat nor a drop of water to drink. That night, the two were forced to go to bed without supper.

The Horse and the Colt

The next day, when they were nearly exhausted with hunger, they were glad to find a few thorny bushes to munch. This time there was no galloping with joy, and after two days, the colt could scarcely drag one leg after the other, he was so hungry.

That night, the horse kept the colt trudging along. In the pitch black, they came to a field of fresh grass. The colt ran at it eagerly. "Oh, what a delicious banquet!" he exclaimed. "Was there ever anything so sweet and tender?

My father, we will seek no further, let us not return to our old home – let's live forever in this lovely spot!"

As he spoke, the day began to break and the colt recognized his surroundings – he was back in their old meadow! Realizing the lesson his father had taught him, he cast down his eyes in shame. But his father merely said, "My child, in future remember this lesson – he who enjoys too much can become fed up of pleasure. To be happy, one must have not too much and not too little."

The Horse and the Olive

An ancient Greek myth retold
by James Baldwin

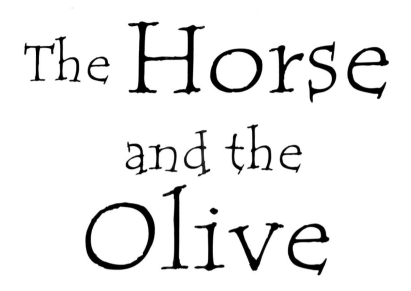

ON A STEEP, STONY HILL in ancient
Greece there once lived some very
poor people who had not yet learned to
build houses. They made their homes in
little caves, which they dug in the earth or
hollowed out among the rocks. Their food

was the flesh of wild animals, which they hunted in the woods, with now and then a few berries or nuts. They did not even know how to make bows and arrows, but used slings and clubs and sharp sticks for weapons, and the little clothing they had was made of skins.

They lived on the top of the hill, because they were safe there from savage beasts and the wild men who roamed through the land. The hill was so steep on every side that there was no way of climbing it – save by a single narrow footpath, which was always guarded by someone at the top.

One day when the men were hunting in the woods, they found a strange youth whose face was so fair and who was dressed

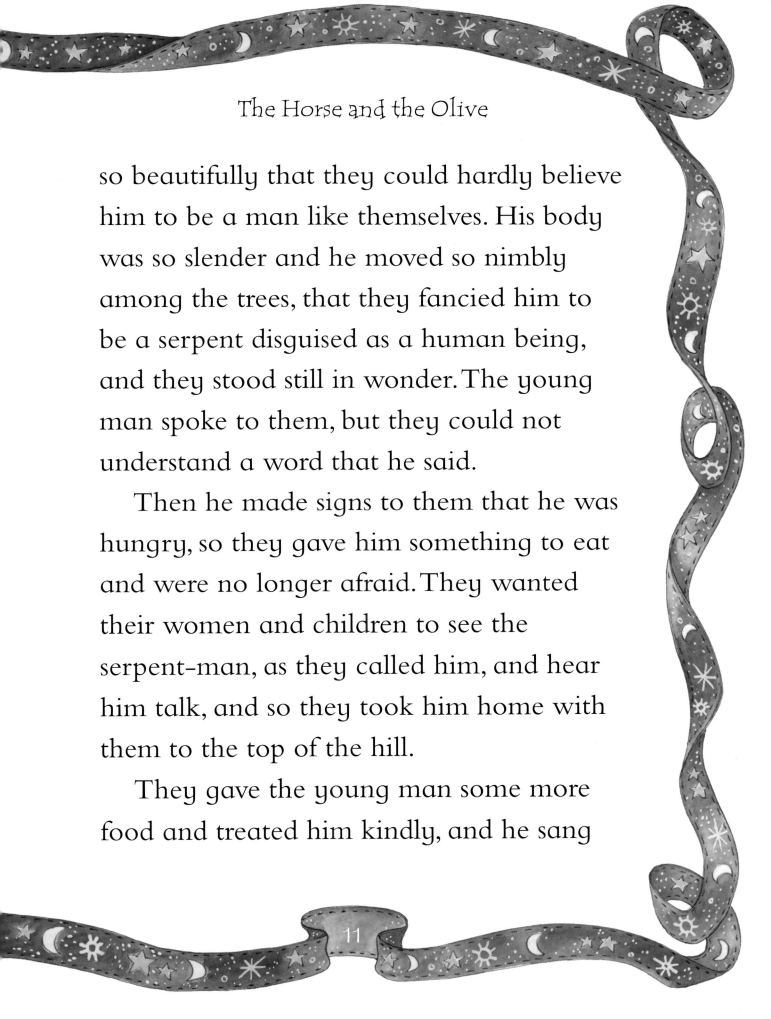

so beautifully that they could hardly believe him to be a man like themselves. His body was so slender and he moved so nimbly among the trees, that they fancied him to be a serpent disguised as a human being, and they stood still in wonder. The young man spoke to them, but they could not understand a word that he said.

Then he made signs to them that he was hungry, so they gave him something to eat and were no longer afraid. They wanted their women and children to see the serpent-man, as they called him, and hear him talk, and so they took him home with them to the top of the hill.

They gave the young man some more food and treated him kindly, and he sang songs to them and talked with their children, and made them happier than they had been for many a day. In a short time he learned to talk in their language, and he told them that his name was Cecrops, and that he had been shipwrecked on the coast not far away, and then he told them many strange things about the land from which he had come and to which he would never be able to return.

The poor people listened and wondered, and it was not long until they began to love him and to look up to him as one wiser than themselves. So Cecrops the serpent-man became the king of the poor people on the hill. He taught them how to make bows and arrows, how to set nets for birds, and how to catch fish with hooks. He led them against the savage wild men of the woods and helped them kill the fierce beasts there. He showed them how to build wooden houses and to thatch them with reeds. And he taught them about the great god Jupiter and the Mighty Folk who lived amid the clouds on the mountain top.

By and by, instead of the wretched caves among the rocks, there was a little town on the top of the hill, with a strong wall and a single narrow gate just where the footpath began to descend to the plain. But as yet the place had no name.

One morning, two strangers were seen in the street. Nobody could tell how they came there. The guard at the gate had not

seen them, and no man had ever dared to climb the narrow footway without his leave. But there the two strangers stood.

One was a man, the other a woman, and they were so tall, and their faces were so grand and noble, that those who saw them stood still and wondered silently.

The man wore a robe of purple and green and he bore in one hand a strong staff with three sharp spear points at one end.

The Horse and the Olive

The woman was not beautiful, but she had wonderful grey eyes, and in one hand she carried a spear and in the other a shield of curious workmanship.

"What is the name of this town?" asked the man. An old man answered, "It has no name. This hill used to be called Cranae, but since King Cecrops arrived, we have been too busy to think of a new name for it."

"Where is this King Cecrops?" asked the strange woman.

"He is in the marketplace with the wise men," said the people, as they watched the two visitors in wonder.

"Lead us to him at once," said the man.

When Cecrops saw the two strangers coming into the marketplace, he stood up to listen. The man spoke first.

"I am Neptune," said he. "I rule the sea."

"I am Athena," said the woman, "and I give wisdom to people."

"I have come to help you make your town a great city," said Neptune. "Give my name to the place, and let me be your protector and patron, and the wealth of the whole world shall be yours. Ships from every land shall bring you gold and silver, and you shall be the masters of the sea."

"My uncle makes you fair promises," said Athena, "but listen to me. Give my name to

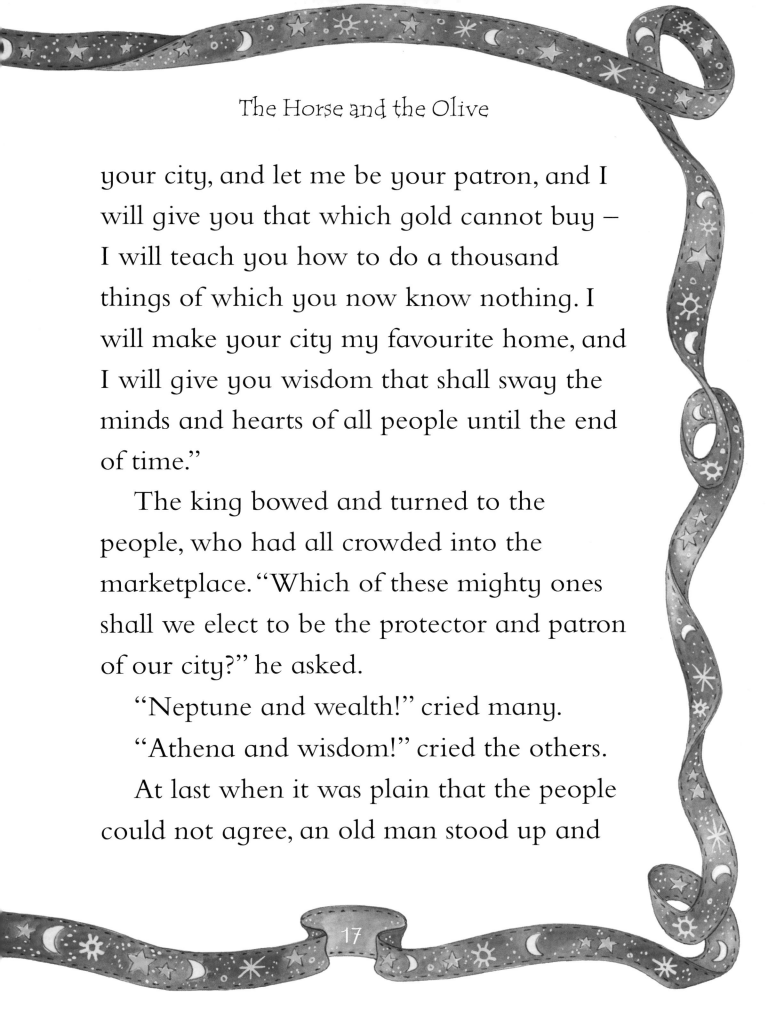

your city, and let me be your patron, and I will give you that which gold cannot buy – I will teach you how to do a thousand things of which you now know nothing. I will make your city my favourite home, and I will give you wisdom that shall sway the minds and hearts of all people until the end of time."

The king bowed and turned to the people, who had all crowded into the marketplace. "Which of these mighty ones shall we elect to be the protector and patron of our city?" he asked.

"Neptune and wealth!" cried many.

"Athena and wisdom!" cried the others.

At last when it was plain that the people could not agree, an old man stood up and said, "These mighty ones have only given us promises — and who knows which is best? Now, if they would only give us some real gift, right now and right here, which we can see, we would know better how to choose."

"That is true!" cried the people.

"Very well, then," said the strangers, "we will each give you a gift, right now, and then you may choose between us."

Neptune gave the first gift. He stood on the highest point of a hill, raised his three-pointed spear high in the air, and then brought it down with great force on a rock. In a flash, a yawning crevice appeared, out of which there sprang a wonderful creature, white as milk, with long slender legs, an arching neck, and a mane and tail of silk.

The people had never seen anything like it before, and they thought it a new kind of bear or wolf or wild boar. Some of them ran and hid in their houses, while others grasped their weapons in alarm. But when they saw the creature stand quietly by the side of Neptune, they lost their fear and came closer to admire its beauty.

"This is my gift," said Neptune. "This animal will carry your burdens for you, he will draw your chariots, he will pull your wagons and your ploughs, he will let you sit on his back and will run with you faster than the wind."

"What is his name?" asked the king.

"His name is Horse," answered Neptune.

Then Athena came forwards. She stood

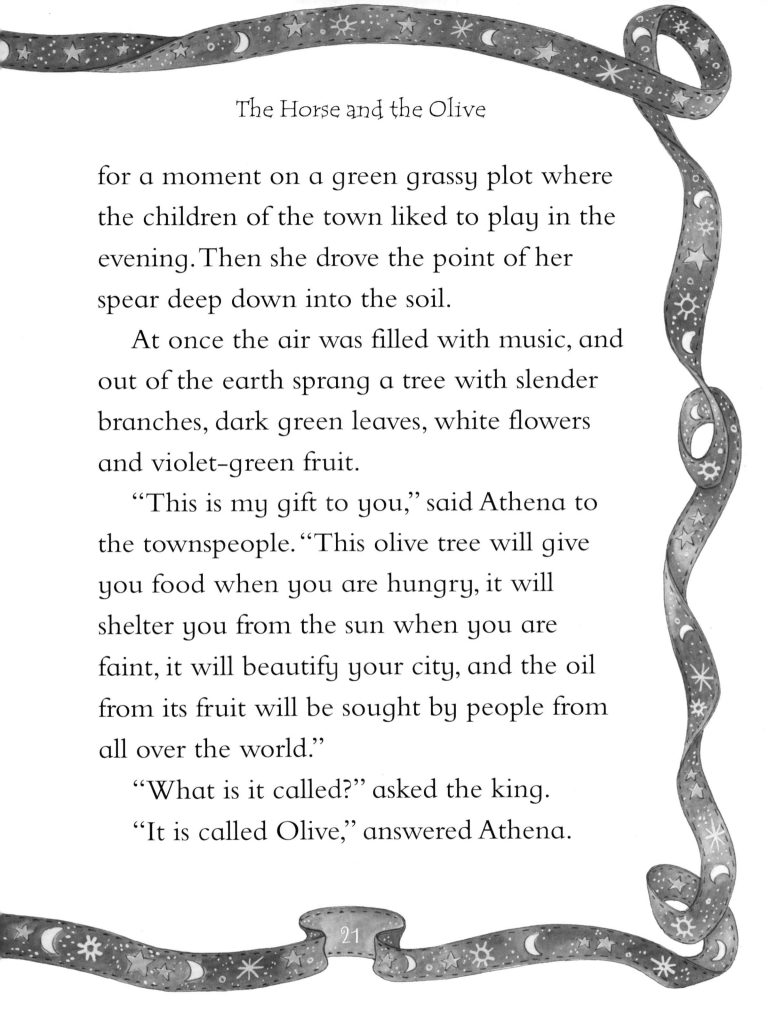

for a moment on a green grassy plot where the children of the town liked to play in the evening. Then she drove the point of her spear deep down into the soil.

At once the air was filled with music, and out of the earth sprang a tree with slender branches, dark green leaves, white flowers and violet-green fruit.

"This is my gift to you," said Athena to the townspeople. "This olive tree will give you food when you are hungry, it will shelter you from the sun when you are faint, it will beautify your city, and the oil from its fruit will be sought by people from all over the world."

"What is it called?" asked the king.

"It is called Olive," answered Athena.

Then the king and his wise men began to talk about the two gifts.

"I do not see that the horse will be of much use to us," said an old man. "As for chariots and wagons and ploughs, we have none of them, and indeed we do not even know what they are. Who among us will ever want to sit on this creature's back and be borne faster than the wind? But the olive tree will be a thing of beauty and a joy for us and our children for years to come."

"Which shall we choose?" asked the king, turning to the people.

"Athena has given us the best gift," they all cried, "we choose Athena and wisdom!"

"Be it so," said the king, "and the name of our city shall be Athens."

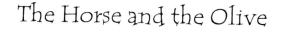

The Horse and the Olive

From that day the town grew and spread, and soon there was not enough room on the hilltop for all the people. When this happened, houses were built in the plain around the foot of the hill, and a great, long road was built to the sea, three miles away. In all the world there was no city more fair than Athens.

In the old marketplace on the top of the hill the people built a temple to Athena, the ruins of which may still be seen. The wonderful olive tree grew and grew and its fruits nourished the town. Many other olive trees sprang from it across Greece, and in all the other countries around the great sea.

As for the horse, he wandered far away across the plains towards the north and

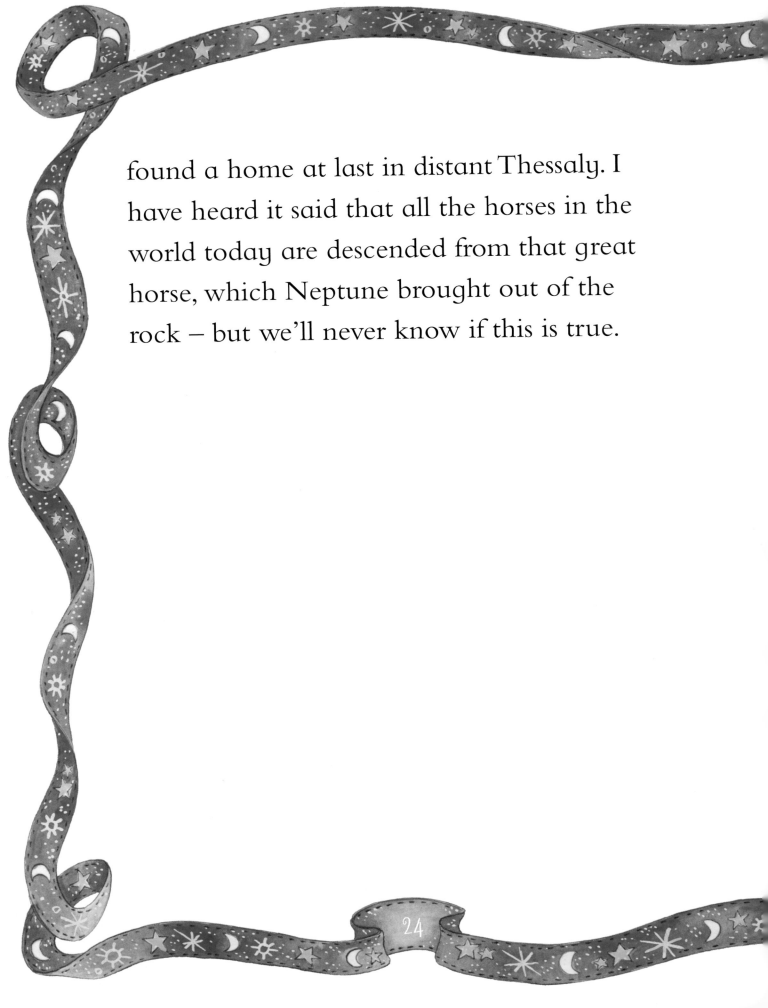

found a home at last in distant Thessaly. I have heard it said that all the horses in the world today are descended from that great horse, which Neptune brought out of the rock — but we'll never know if this is true.

Winding-up Time

From *Mopsa the Fairy* by Jean Ingelow

In this story, a boy called Jack finds a nest of fairies in a hollow thorn tree. By magic, he journeys on the back of an albatross, a huge seabird, and then by boat to Fairyland…

JACK LOOKED at the hot brown rocks on the riverbank until he was quite tired, but at last the shore became flat. He saw a beautiful little bay where the water was still, and where the grass grew down to the water's edge.

He was so pleased that he cried out hastily, "Oh, how I wish my boat would go into that bay and let me land!"

Jack had no sooner spoke than the boat altered its course, as if somebody had been steering her, and began to make for the bay as fast as she could go.

'How very odd!' thought Jack.

As they drew closer to the bay the water became so shallow that you could see crabs and lobsters walking about on the bottom. At last the boat's keel grated on the pebbles.

Just as Jack began to think of jumping onto the shore, he saw two little old women approaching. They were gently driving a white horse before them. The horse had baskets on each of its sides, and the women

looked like
washer-women.

Jack jumped out of the boat and said to
one of the old women, "Please can you tell
me if this is Fairyland?"

"What did he say?" asked one old
woman of the other.

"He said, 'Is this Fairyland?'" replied the other, who began to empty the baskets of small shirts, coats and stockings. When the women had made them into two little heaps they knelt down and began to wash them in the river, taking no further notice of Jack whatsoever.

Jack stared at them. They were not much taller than himself and they were not taking the slightest care of their clothes. Then he looked at the white horse, who was hanging his head over the lovely, clear water with a very discontented air.

At last the first washer-woman said, "I shall leave off now – I've got a pain."

"Do," said the other. "We'll go home and have a cup of tea."

The washer-women wrung out the clothes, put them into the baskets again and, taking the old horse by the bridle, began gently to lead him away.

Jack sprang ashore and said to the boat, "Stay just where you are, will you?" and he ran after the old women, calling to them, "Is there any law to prevent my coming into your country?"

"Woah!" cried the first old woman and the horse stopped, while the second woman repeated, "Any law? No, not that I know of — but if you are a stranger here you had better look out."

"Why?" asked Jack.

"You don't suppose, do you," one of the washer-women said to the other, "that our

queen will wind up strangers?"

While Jack was wondering what she meant, the other said, "I shouldn't wonder if he lasts eight days. Gee!" and the horse went on.

"No, woah!" said the other woman.

"No, no. Gee! I tell you," cried the first.

Upon this, to Jack's astonishment, the old horse stopped, and said, "Now, then, which is it to be? I'm willing to gee, and I'm agreeable to woah, but what's a horse to do when you say both together?"

"Why, he talks!" said Jack.

"Yes, it's because he's got a head cold," observed one of the washer-women. "He always talks when he's got a cold, and there's no pleasing him. Whatever you say, he's just not satisfied. Gee, Boney, do!"

"Gee it is, then," said the horse, and it began to jog on.

"He spoke again!" said Jack and the horse laughed. Jack was quite alarmed.

"It appears that horses from your land don't talk?" observed the first woman.

"Never," answered Jack, "they can't."

"You mean they won't," observed the horse. And though he spoke the words of mankind, it was in a different voice. Jack felt that the horse's voice was just the natural tone for a horse and that it did not arise

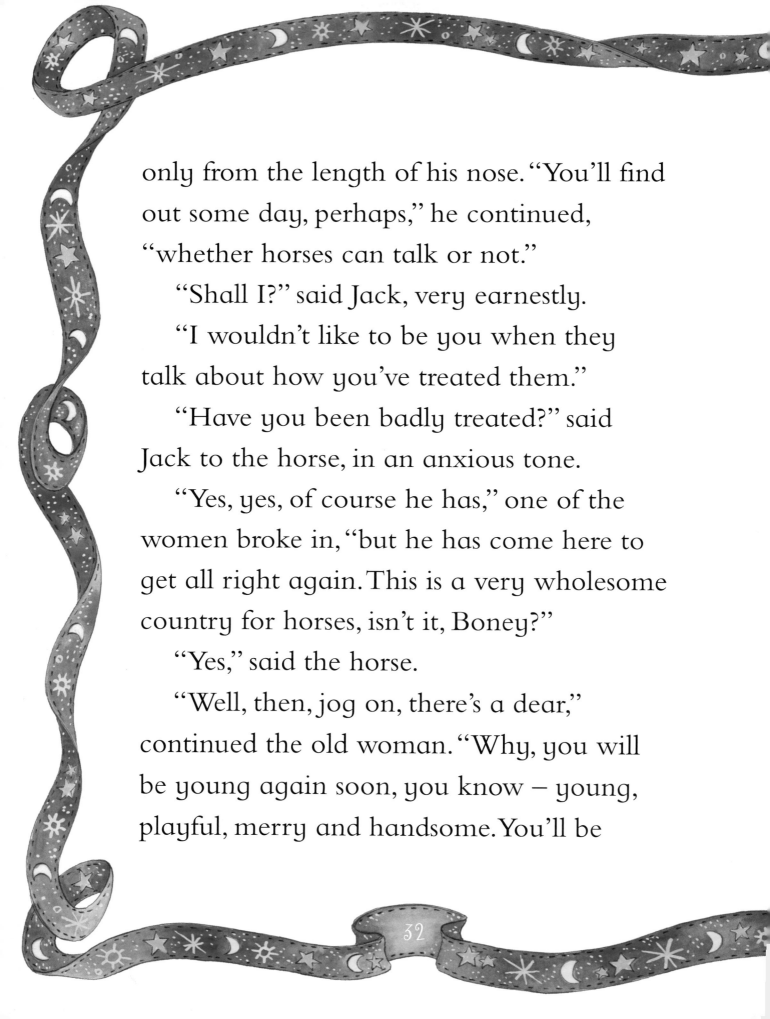

only from the length of his nose. "You'll find out some day, perhaps," he continued, "whether horses can talk or not."

"Shall I?" said Jack, very earnestly.

"I wouldn't like to be you when they talk about how you've treated them."

"Have you been badly treated?" said Jack to the horse, in an anxious tone.

"Yes, yes, of course he has," one of the women broke in, "but he has come here to get all right again. This is a very wholesome country for horses, isn't it, Boney?"

"Yes," said the horse.

"Well, then, jog on, there's a dear," continued the old woman. "Why, you will be young again soon, you know – young, playful, merry and handsome. You'll be quite a colt, by and by, and then we shall set you free to join your companions in the happy meadows."

The old horse was so comforted by this kind speech that he pricked up his ears and quickened his pace considerably.

"Pray, are you a boy?" asked the second old woman.

"Yes," said Jack, as he skipped along to keep up.

"A real boy, that doesn't need winding up?" inquired the old woman.

"I don't know what you mean," answered Jack, "but I am a real boy, certainly."

"Ah!" she replied. "I thought you were, by the way Boney spoke to you. Real people worked Boney hard, and often drove him about all night in the miserable streets, and never let him have so much as a canter in a green field," said one of the women, "but he'll be all right now, only he has to begin at the wrong end."

"What do you mean?" said Jack.

"Why, in this country," answered the old woman, "the horses begin by being terribly old and stiff, and they seem miserable at first, but slowly they get young again, as you heard me reminding him."

"Indeed," said Jack, "and do you like it that way?"

"It has nothing to do with me," she answered. "We are here to take care of all the creatures men have ill used. They are very sick and old when first they come to us. But then we take care of them and gradually bring them up to be young and happy once more."

"This must be a very nice country to live in, then," said Jack.

"For horses it is," said the old lady, significantly.

"Well," said Jack, "it does seem very full of haystacks, certainly, and all the air smells just like fresh grass."

At this moment they came to a beautiful, wildflower meadow, and the old horse stopped, and, turning to the first woman, said, "Faxa, I think I could fancy a handful of clover."

Upon this, Faxa snatched Jack's cap off

his head, jumped over a little ditch, and gathering some clover, presently brought it back full, handing it to the old horse with great civility.

"You shouldn't be in such a hurry," observed the old horse, "you'll wind down if you don't take care."

Just then, a little man dressed like a groom came running up, out of breath. "Come along! I hear the bell, and we are a good way from the palace!"

Jack heard a bell ringing violently from some distance away, and when the groom began to run, he ran beside him.

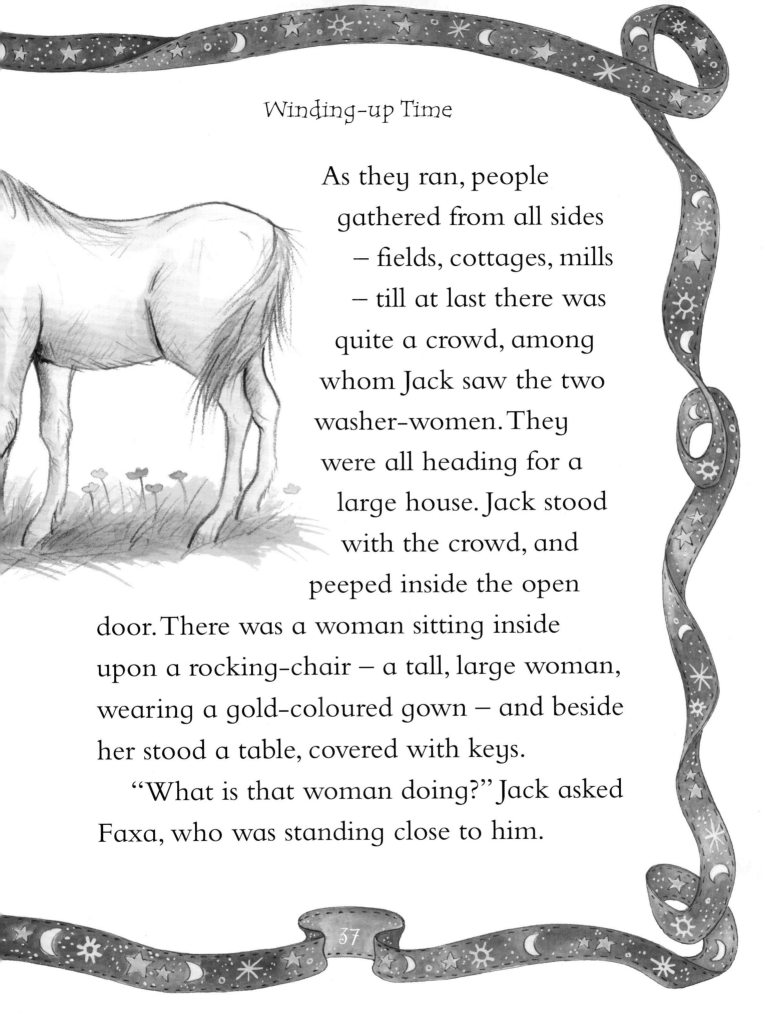

As they ran, people gathered from all sides – fields, cottages, mills – till at last there was quite a crowd, among whom Jack saw the two washer-women. They were all heading for a large house. Jack stood with the crowd, and peeped inside the open door. There was a woman sitting inside upon a rocking-chair – a tall, large woman, wearing a gold-coloured gown – and beside her stood a table, covered with keys.

"What is that woman doing?" Jack asked Faxa, who was standing close to him.

"Winding us up, to be sure," answered Faxa. "You don't suppose, surely, that we can go on for ever?"

"Extraordinary!" said Jack. "Are you wound up every evening, like watches?"

"Unless we have misbehaved ourselves," she answered, "and then she lets us run right the way down."

"And what then?"

"Why, then we have to stop and stand against a wall, till she is pleased to forgive us, and let our friends carry us in to be wound up again."

Jack looked in. He saw the people enter and stand close by the woman. One after the other she took them by the chin with her left hand and with her right hand found a key that pleased her. It seemed to Jack that there was a tiny keyhole in the back of their heads, and that she put the key in to wind them up.

"You must take your turn with the others," said the groom.

"There's no keyhole in my head," said Jack, "I don't want anyone to wind me up."

"But you must do as others do," he persisted, "and if you have no keyhole, our queen can easily have one made."

"Make one in my head!" exclaimed Jack. "She shall do no such thing!"

"We shall see," said Faxa, quietly. Jack was so frightened that he ran back towards the river as fast as his legs would carry him. Many of the people called to him to stop, but they could not run after him, because they wanted winding up. They would certainly have caught him if he had not been very quick, for before he got to the river he heard the footsteps of the queen's attendants. He sprang into the boat just before they reached the edge of the water.

As soon as he jumped aboard, the boat moved out into the middle of the stream. Jack did not feel safe until there was a long stretch of water between him and the shore.

By this time he began to feel very tired and sleepy, so he laid down in the bottom of the boat, and fell into a doze, and then into a dream.